JOY

notionpress
.com

JOY

PROSENJIT
ADHYA

(This Book has Adult Content)

notionpress.com

Notion Press

Old No. 38, New No. 6
McNichols Road, Chetpet
Chennai - 600 031

First Published by Notion Press 2016

ISBN 978-93-86009-15-9

Contents

INTRODUCTION

In today's world, there are people with different kinds of personalities. Some have inherent instincts that dominate in them, leading them to actions that brand them as belonging to a particular category. They are engineers, doctors or businessmen. But, there are some incidents that happen in our lives that can change us completely, or can have an effect on our personalities. Such incidents are embedded in our brains. They lead us to reflect on them again and again. As we do so, our actions follow.

It is very important that the upbringing of an individual should be done carefully and in a homely environment from childhood. The human brain is very receptive. All incidents or happenings that take place have a direct impact on us. In other words, we respond and act according to various incidents that happen around us. We learn what we see, and listen to all that happens in our everyday lives.

It is more relevant in today's world, where in our day-to-day activities, from start to end; we are exposed to various incidents that make us respond as multiple people, or as multiple characters. A normal life would have defined roles for different entities and people: a father, son, brother, friend and above all, the person himself, as the sole entity.

One can resemble his mother, father or anyone in the family in certain ways that we define as natural behaviour inherited genetically. There is an exception when we come across personalities who are born geniuses. Their parents may have led normal lives. When we define "normal life," we mean that it is an average life with every person being drawn into a routine, daily life. One has an average span of sixty years from childhood to retirement.

When we move out of a "normal life" and do something different that is not accepted by society, the question then arises as to whether there is an imbalance or not. Is it possible that there is a completely different person who leads a normal life? A side that is not known to the world? A person that is completely in the dark and not exposed to the external world?

Does society allow a person to have two totally different lives? I don't think it is possible. Some of the world's greatest newsmakers have been in this category, with a few extremities on the good and the bad side. It is all because of the hormones in us. We are not in control of ourselves, many times, just because of what I call as the basic instinct. The brain which controls all our actions, fails.

The other side of the story is how a personality is termed as a split personality and has been exposed to situations from childhood, which makes him a genius or a pariah in the normal world.

I would like to stress on this particular category of two personalities in a person, and the contrast to maintain the balance between the two. The character in this book leads a normal life and is balanced, but is driven by strong hormonal basic instincts.

JOY LIVES TWO LIVES. THIS BOOK IS AN ILLUSTRATION OF BOTH HIS LIVES.

THE EARLY DAYS

It was in the early seventies. Joy was a growing child, playing in the garden in his paternal grandparents' house. He was just eight. His grandfather was passing the ball to him. They were in the lush green courtyard of the ancient house in an eastern state of India. Joy was their only grandson and the family was well known. They enjoyed a life of grandeur. After a while, his grandfather had to attend to some appointments and called the maid to take care of Joy. It was already nearing noon. There was no one in the house, except for grandmother and the maid.

The parents had gone out for a gathering with some friends. His grandmother was busy preparing lunch in the kitchen. The two-storey house had six rooms on the ground floor and windows opening out onto the garden. Seema, the maid was young and caring. She took the ball in her hands, and started playing with Joy. Grandfather had already left by then. After some time, Kailash the (gardener) arrived. He approached Seema and started talking to her. Within a few minutes, Seema left Joy on the portico and approached one of the rooms of the house that had an open window, which looked straight out into the garden. Joy was all alone. He was busy playing with the ball. He did not realize that Seema had left him. In a few minutes Joy was all alone and Seema was not to be seen. The gardener was also not around. She and the gardener were not in the portico, either. The ball rolled towards the room. Joy went chasing after it. As he searched for it, he heard the voice of Seema from the window. He heard her moaning, Joy was confused and did not dare to call her to search for the ball. He slowly went towards the window and peeped in to it see if it was her. He was shocked and confused to see the state in which the gardener and Seema were in.

They were both naked. Joy couldn't understand what was happening. He was quiet and afraid, but watched the scene before him. The gardener had his hands on the maid's breasts. Joy could see her well developed breasts and the black circle with nipples that popped out. Seema was moaning and the gardener started to lick her breasts and pressing them. She held the gardener tight against her body and laid her hands on his buttocks. Her breasts were big. By this time, the gardener had started sucking them. She spread her legs apart and her hairy pussy was visible. The gardener's penis was large. Seema was massaging it as he moaned. The pink head of the organ was visible. Seema spread her legs wider.

Seema and Kailash were at the peak of excitement. She took his hand and put it on her hairy bottom. Kailash inserted his finger into her vagina. It was pink, and Joy could see the hole. All of a sudden, Kailash pulled back. He turned around and put his erect and large organ into Seema's mouth.

Seema gave Kailash a blow job, while he was licking and sucking Seema's clitoris. She was wet and excited. Kailash turned around, and inserted his organ into Seema's. He started moving back and forth. Both of them were wild. Seema crossed her legs around Kailash's buttocks. She gripped him tight with her hands. They soon began moaning together. Seema seemed to be at the peak of excitement. Joy was spellbound by all this. Suddenly, Seema flipped over, and Joy saw her buttocks. They were big. He could see her arse. Kailash began to lick it, and was caressing her wildly. His already large organ seemed to have attained its maximum size. Seema's buttocks were fair and had pink splotches as she bent over before Kailash. He inserted his penis from behind. Seema moaned as Kailash moved back and forth. Seema was moaning, and all of a sudden, Kailash pulled out his penis. A milky fluid was seen flowing out of it. Immediately, Seema turned around and took the entire fluid into her mouth. She was smiling. Both of them seemed satisfied. Joy was sweating by this time. It was like a scene from a movie. It was time for Seema and Kailash to leave, but Kailash pulled her to him and kissed her. He put his tongue into Seema's mouth and kissed her deeply. Seema then went to the bathroom and Kailash began to put on his clothes.

Poor little Joy! He slowly climbed down the window and totally forgot about the ball. He walked through the garden and tried to figure out what it was that he had seen. As he approached to the portico, Seema and Kailash had gotten out of the room. "Where were you, Joy?" asked Seema. Joy could not look into Seema's eyes. He had seen her naked. Speechless and nervous, he slowly asked Seema, Where was she, and told her that he needed her to search for the ball. Joy couldn't shake off what he saw. He couldn't stop thinking of Seema's hairy parts. Later, he asked Seema's, for her permission to go to his grandmother.

Instead of going to his grandmother, Joy went upstairs. The scene he had watched now kept playing over and over in his mind. As he went upstairs, he heard his grandmother calling out to him. He was to take his bath and then go for lunch. Usually, Seema gave him a bath. She came upstairs and took Joy to the bathroom. She undressed him and got him ready for his bath. As Seema touched him, for the first time, Joy sensed a different feeling. The young lad's eyes were on Seema's cleavage as she bent over. He got excited as Seema rubbed him down with soap and poured water on his body. For the first time ever, he had a different feeling. Seema was beautiful. She was an attractive woman, twenty-four years old. Joy was a little boy of just eight. After his bath, Joy was ready for lunch, but his eye was on Seema, who also managed kitchen work. Joy sat for lunch, watching Seema. Again, it was Seema who took care of him while he ate. As he ate, his parents arrived. Joy was happy to see them.

He could not express what he had seen to anyone. At his age, he could have asked what it was that he had seen, but he did not do so. In his early childhood, Joy had seen what he should have not seen. After lunch, Seema took Joy for his afternoon nap in his bedroom. She then went for her bath. She usually tended to undress herself partially in front of Joy, and didn't think much of it considering his age. But this time, she was not aware that Joy had seen her naked. As he was about to close his eyes, Seema removed her saree and went to the bathroom. Joy could not sleep. He was inclined on seeing Seema naked. As a young boy, his senses were growing. He was still too young to understand and sense his rise into adulthood. Joy was in the Third Standard, and studied in a co-educational school. It was a Sunday when all this had happened. The next day was Monday and Joy had to go to school the next day.

That evening, he sat down with his books to study. But thoughts of Seema had not gone away as he replayed her movements and her moans in his mind. He was developing a strong sense of attraction towards the scene he had seen that morning.

It was a sunny Monday morning. Joy went to school as usual. He was the favourite of all the teachers and most of them were women. Joy was the most enthusiastic student in class and popular amongst all, teachers and students alike. The first class was English. His teacher had worn a beautiful saree and a sleeveless blouse. Being a first bencher, he often got the most attention. As class started, the teacher pointed at Joy and said, "Yes! Joy, I am sure you have done your homework!" Of course, he had done it. He was very attentive in class. Every move of the teacher reminded Joy of Seema. He began to fascinate his teacher, as he went into a different world. "Yes? Joy, have you understood this paragraph?" asked the teacher. Joy was clever enough to answer. "Yes Ma'am!" he answered. He glanced at his teacher's buttocks as she turned around to face the blackboard. Seema's, was in his mind. When class ended, Joy returned to his real world.

The Encounter

Months went by. Joy was growing up and Seema was always a fascination to him. She was the real woman for him. By the time he got into his teenage years and attained puberty, Seema was still working at his house and had kids, and was happily married. She used to call him "Joy Baba." Being the best in class, Joy enjoyed all the privilege in the family circle and at school. But, by now, he started getting more and more interested in elderly women rather than women of his own age. He was in Class IX. He had begun learning about sex. Sex Education was a subject in his curriculum.

Having attained puberty, Joy had developed his senses and organs. He could feel the changes in his body. He had begun getting wet dreams. He started having night flows. Seema was the object of his fascination and that led him to masturbate. He had not forgotten what he had seen six years ago. He was now tall and handsome with a faint trace of a beard. He had some pubic hair on his private parts. He was growing into a man. Just two years left, and he would be giving his Board Exams.

Joy had always restricted himself to books and maintained his habit of reading to be the best in class. He had a lot of girlfriends but none of them interested him.

It was Seema that Joy craved for. He wanted to have a sexual encounter with her. Seema had just stepped in her thirties, and Joy was only a growing boy in the teens. One fine morning, Joy was about to get dressed for school. He was naked when Seema entered the room, looking for him. Seema saw him naked with the few grown hairs on his body. She noticed the faint traces of pubic hair near his penis. She was shocked and turned away, pretending that she had not seen Joy. There was no one in the house except for his grandparents. His parents had gone out. Joy lost his senses and caught hold of Seema's hand. He hugged her tight. Seema wanted to get out of it. "Please!" she said. Seema, a grown woman, knew that Joy was doing something wrong. He was a teenager and was in the growing stage.

"You are going to be late for school!" said Seema.

"Seema, No!" said Joy. He turned Seema around and kissed her on her lips. His penis was hard and erect and he held onto Seema's saree. She was struggling to loosen his grip, as Joy finally took his hand and put it on her back and pressed her buttocks hard.

"Listen!" he said, and narrated the entire scene that he saw six years ago. Seema was spellbound and could not believe what she was hearing. She was afraid that someone would see them. She kept saying, "Joy Baba, this is not right!" As a matured woman, she understood Joy's feelings and found that he was deeply fascinated and infatuated with her. She knew he wanted to have sex with her, and she wanted to get out of his grasp. Joy was out of control and took Seema's hand, and put it on his

THE EXCURSION

The Higher Secondary exams were over. Joy was now preparing for his competitive exams. He had already started his tuitions and was a fair and handsome looking boy. Girls were fond of him, but he was always driven towards older women. Joy was a decent guy and was well adored amongst his friends, classmates and family. He turned out to be the best in class, as an all rounder. Joy was in the Science Group and was preparing for his Medical and Engineering exams. It was time for the annual excursion at school. Everyone had planned for an excursion to Manali. All the teachers were accompanying the students on the excursion. There were both, male and female teachers, who had planned the trip.

The day for their departure to Manali had arrived. Everyone was ready to leave. They boarded the train on time. There was fun and joy in the air. The train moved towards its destination. At night, it hot as it was summer. Joy got up to go to the toilet. As he approached one of the toilets, he noticed that the door to one was ajar, and he opened it. He found his teacher inside, urinating. She looked up and saw him. She was shocked. Joy noticed that her pussy was clean shaven. He went in and closed the door behind him. The teacher told him to lock the door as she stood up. She slowly put her hand on Joy's crotch and undid the zip. She pressed his penis. Taking Joy's hand, she moved it over her pussy. She was in her mid-thirties and was fair. Her pussy and protruding clit were pink. She put her hand down Joy's pants, and pulled his underwear down. She took out his penis. She asked Joy to hold her tight, and Joy did, pressing down on her bottom. It was soft. Joy was experiencing a unique. She was like butter: beautiful and smooth.

The teacher bent down and took Joy's penis into her mouth and began sucking it. Joy could not resist it. But, it was an Indian-styled bathroom in the train and not much could be done. He was strong, and after his teacher had given him the blow job, he took his teacher onto his thighs in a standing position, holding her back. He began to push his penis into her vagina. It was pink and wet. She was excited and her eyes showed that she wanted sex hungrily. He moved back and forth and her weight was on Joy's legs. He had the stamina and fucked her hard and finally ejaculated into her vagina. She relaxed, and then wanted him to suck her breasts. As she exposed her breasts, he noticed that they were big. Her nipples were pink. He took one breast by hand pressed it hard, and then sucked the nipples. She had recently delivered a baby, and Joy found milk spurting out of her nipples. As he pressed the nipples, the milk sprayed out and he drank whatever came out. It was an experience by itself and his face was full of milk. Her breasts were wet. It was 3:00 AM. Everyone was asleep on their berths. She was fair and beautiful. Joy's fascinations were growing. Joy was moving towards a life where he was driven more by sex than anything else. He had never touched girls of his age. This was the second lady with whom he had such an encounter. He was not a playboy, but his encounters were only with older women. He was now experienced, having had sex many times. Many boys at his age did not have that. The urge for more and more sex was growing in him. He was not keen on masturbating, as he was getting the real thing in real life.

Two days after the encounter on the train, Joy had sex with his teacher again, this time in a hotel room, when the others were out trekking. She was completely naked and was on top of Joy. She sat on his penis and started licking his body all over. She moved her buttocks back and forth. Her vagina was wet and the fluid was pouring out. Joy held her buttocks and sucked her nipples. She was on top of him, with his penis inside her. For the first time, someone had asked Joy to have anal sex. She turned around and opened up her anus. It was pink. Joy's penis was large and erect. He licked his teacher's arse and inserted his fingers into it. She was moaning. She wanted more. He put his spit on her anus and started licking it. Joy had never done this dirty job before, but his teacher had asked for it. She had already leaked the white fluid from her vagina and Joy was already taking it into his mouth. It was raw sex. He inserted his penis into her anus and pushed it deep inside. He could hear her moan, and she was enjoying every moment.

His teacher's buttocks were round and big. Her curves were fantastic. It was like heaven on earth, for Joy, and for the kind of sex that he was having with her was amazing. As he was thrust into her, someone knocked on the door. It was another teacher called Shalini. She was in her early twenties. Nervous, Joy was hesitant to open the door. But hearing the voice, his teacher told Joy that it was okay, since it was Shalini and she could come in. Joy opened the door. Shalini was shocked to see the teacher naked, but an offer was made to her to have sex with Joy. Joy had wrapped a towel around his waist. His penis was erect and large. The teacher asked Shalini to remove his towel. She was hesitant, but she did so and was excited to see the size of Joy's penis. Shalini was of a light build. She pressed Joy's penis hard and took his red head into her mouth. She gave him a blow job. By this time, Shalini was naked. She had a hairy pussy with a vagina that was brown and black. Her nipples were black and her breasts were medium-sized. Her buttocks were average and she was slim. Joy was now satisfying two women at one time. His teacher was licking Joy's buttocks. Joy pressed Shalini's nipples as she gave him the blowjob. Shalini was excited. She wanted Joy to fuck her hard. There was no seduction from Shalini as Joy was already seduced by his teacher. Both of them took turns to get fucked in different styles. Shalini enjoyed it. Joy licked her arse which was black. Finally, Joy ejaculated. Both of them took his cum and Joy was now a hero to both of them. It was time to leave and three of them took a shower naked and there were many kisses exchanged.

There was a big change in Joy now. Though he was leading a normal life, his sex life was dominating his normal life. This was dangerous, as he was now at a turning point in his life, and would have to decide the course of his career. The Higher Secondary results were declared and Joy had topped the class. Both teachers were happy with his performance in their subjects, and the experience

Joy shared with them during the excursion. It was time for Joy to bid goodbye to school and join college.

Joy got into an Engineering College where career prospects were bright for him. Now, he was more matured and had gathered experience through sexual encounters from the day he met Seema in bed. Again, he was not attracted to any girls of his age.

It was the first year in Engineering College. Everyone had high expectations. Joy was congratulated by every teacher in college for his brilliant performances. Two years went by and all of a sudden, a twist entered Joy's life. He met his first girlfriend in college. This time, it was his classmate. Could Joy get into a relationship, after his past experiences?

The Meeting

It was the third year in Engineering College. Mala had entered Joy's life. She used to share every moment with the handsome Joy. He was the best in class and was very caring. They went on dates, and watched movies together. Parties were common and the whole college knew them to be lovers. Was Joy in love with Mala? Or was she just a friend? He had to face this someday or the other.

It was the Final Year. On Mala's birthday, Joy gave her a wonderful gift. After the party she hosted, everyone left. Mala had something to decide upon, with Joy. She loved him but till date, they had not had sex with each other. Joy was a decent guy and cared for her. Mala proposed not to return to the hostel and instead, that night, she had booked a hotel room for both of them to spend together. This was a surprise to Joy.

Mala asked Joy if he was afraid. "Do you love me?" she asked, as she kissed Joy. He had no answer. He was driven by different relationships in the past. His experiences were different. Could he make love to Mala? His past experiences were brave sexual encounters that started with Seema. He stopped for a moment and said yes. Mala's face lit up with joy and then they moved to the hotel. As Mala entered the hotel room, Joy was afraid about whether Mala would ask him to make love to her. In their relationship of two years, he did not ever think of a physical relationship with her. The hotel room was magnificent and Mala had made all the arrangements to spend time with Joy. As they entered the room, Mala took her night-dress and went to the bathroom to change. In the meantime, Joy changed into his nightwear, as well. Mala was deeply in love with Joy and wanted to marry him. Joy already had a job offer from a US-based company and was due to fly to the US in less than six months' time.

Mala came out of the bathroom with a smile. Joy noticed that there was a big difference between his past experiences and the present. He had known all the secrets of a woman and he knew that he would not be able to share his experiences with Mala. He knew that it would lead to a breakup. He had sex many times and each of the times, with women older than him.

Mala lay down on the bed and began talking about different topics. She finally proposed that she was interested in marrying Joy. This struck him like a thunderbolt and he did not expect such a proposal. Mala was in her early twenties. She was fair and beautiful, tall enough to match Joy with a good figure to match. As she proposed to Joy, she moved close to him and laid her hands on his chest. She hugged her and wanted to get the feeling of togetherness with Joy. Joy was nervous and did not intend to have the same kind of an experience as before. But Mala was also a woman. She slowly moved to kiss Joy's lips.

Joy did not respond to it, and it made Mala uncomfortable. She wanted Joy to hug her. She wore a night-dress and her proportionate breasts were partially visible. Joy was in control. She put her breasts close to Joy's chest and put her legs on Joy's legs. Finally, she was forced to ask Joy whether he was interested in having sex. The answer was a no. He felt that he had gotten involved in a different relationship with other women and his personality had changed. Mala felt insulted. She was a balanced lady and she did not force Joy. Neither did she remove her clothes to seduce him. The night passed on and both chatted until it was morning. There was no sex. It was simple that Joy was driven by a different kind of relationship with other women. The next day, Mala met Joy at college as usual. There were no complaints against him. Meanwhile, Joy had decided to marry Mala, primarily because of the night and her approach. Days went by and both of them graduated from their Engineering College with individual job offers. Joy left for the USA after six months and Mala was placed in Bangalore. They were supposed to get married in a year or so with Mala moving to the US with Joy.

The aircraft had just landed in New York and Joy was in a new environment. It was a foreign country and it was his first experience abroad. He was received by a company representative who drove him through the streets of New York to a hotel. It was in the heart of Manhattan. Joy was thrilled and called back home in India to inform them that he had landed safely. Thrilled as they were, for every question they asked, Joy's response was "Sab Thik Thak Hai." After a conversation for almost half-an-hour, Joy disconnected the call and was ready for a shower when the bell rang. He went to the door, in his towel. There was a blonde girl from housekeeping. She had to change some of the toiletry as it was requested by Joy. She was almost 5 ft, six inches tall, with busty buttocks and had big breasts. She had blonde hair and spoke with an American accent. She wore a short skirt. As she bent down to change some of the Toiletry. Joy could see her inner wear, her curves were great. Joy was excited and the room door was closed. This was America and not India. Here, any sort of misbehaviour could cost him his job. Nevertheless, he took a chance and loosened his towel, the girl turned around and saw Joy naked. His penis was already large and erect as he had begun to imagine things. "Oh! Sorry!" said the girl, and held the towel for him to put it back on. She seemed normal, as it was America, and nudity was no surprise. Joy was bold enough to hold her hand and place it on his penis. He then took it to his pubic hair in the region. The girl stood up and was hesitant. But Joy insisted and hugged her. She was a cute babe, and not willing to do what Joy wanted. Joy took his hand on her back and touched her vagina from the bottom. He pulled down her panties. In the meantime, he put his tongue into her mouth and started smooching her. The girl finally gave in. She started to remove her shirt. As she removed it, Joy saw her pink bra, and the cleavage of her breasts. He kissed the cleavage, and slowly removed the bra. She was enticing. Her breasts were fantastic. They were round, big and had pink nipples. The nipples were big, and could be seen even when she had her bra on. Finally, the girl was naked. She had a hairy pussy, blonde and curly. Joy laid his hands on her hairy pussy and urged her to have a shower with him. Her name was Anny. As he hugged her she equally was excited and started massaging Joy's penis. It was a hot water bath for them. As the water sprinkled down the girl's body, Joy started kissing her lower abdomen and her navel. He drank the water that dropped down Anny's body. He started to lick, turned her around and kissed her buttocks. He then opened up her anus and licked it. It was pink and her pussy was equally pink. By this time, Anny was hot and excited. She took her position and took Joy's penis into her mouth, and began giving him a blowjob. She started to move the foreskin of Joy's penis up and down, and then started to take his penis deep into her mouth. She had swallowed most of it. For the first time, Joy found a girl licking his balls. She started to lick and bite them. She stood up for a final shower and then took the towel to wipe the water off. Both of them were now in bed and Joy couldn't resist anymore. He held Anny and spread her legs apart. Her Pussy was pink and her vagina was wet. Both of them exchanged positions and Joy started to lick her pussy. She was excited and moved her body. "Please, I want it in!" Joy took his penis and inserted it into her pink vagina and started to fuck her hard. She put his hands on Joy's buttocks and started moving it back and forth. This was not the end. She turned round and wanted to get fucked in doggy style. She put his penis inside her vagina and Joy started to fuck her. Her buttocks were soft, smooth, and round. The curves were visible. This was over, and now, Joy was in bed, and Anny was on top of him. She sat on his penis and inserted it into her vagina, and started riding him like a horse. It was a peak and better than every other experience Joy had before. He could not hold it longer and the milky white fluid started to gush out of his penis.

Anny did not object to have it inside her vagina. She expressed a sigh of relief when they were both done. As she got up, Joy saw her pussy wet, and cum was flowing down her vagina.

This was Joy's first sexual encounter in the US. He was living a life with women for momentary relationships. Knowing that he would be getting married to Mala in a few months' time, could he resist such relationships? He had to live two lives and two personalities, one with Mala as a husband, and the other with sexual ecstasy involving other women. Anny had a few encounters with Joy in the same hotel room for as long as he stayed.

Six months passed by. Mala was now flying from India to the US with an assignment. Joy had taken an apartment in the heart of Manhattan. Though expensive, he managed to rent it, a studio apartment, Anny moved on with her own life and there was not much contact. Joy was preparing to receive Mala. She was going to be staying with Joy.

Mala

Joy's life was to move around Mala's now as she was moving down from India to the US for a two-year assignment and would be with Joy. Though yet to get married, they enjoyed the freedom of staying together. The final day had arrived when Air Lufthansa landed in New York. Joy was there at the airport to receive Mala and as he moved towards the arrivals, Joy saw Mala waving at him. She was dressed in a pink top and blue jeans. Beautiful as she was, this time looking all the more so, she jumped onto Joy and hugged him, and gave him a kiss. Both of them drove though the busy streets of New York and Mala was thrilled to see the city. She was posted in a Bank in New York as a Data Analyst from her company.

As they reached Joy's apartment, it was already 8:00 PM. New York was lit. From the apartment, a charismatic view of the city was seen. Mala unpacked her luggage and was ready for a shower. This time she undressed herself in front of Joy and was in her underclothing and requested that Joy should join her for a shower. She was beautiful and glamorous and was looking all the more with her red colour bra and dark brown panties. This time, Mala hugged Joy and took him by his hand slid it down her panties and Joy could feel the hairy pussy. She took it down. She had taken his hand into her vagina. Mala was a virgin. As she inserted Joy's finger she felt the pain. Joy was now losing control and his penis had already begun to respond. Mala was wet by this time. She could feel Joy's penis growing large. She finally held his penis and started moving her hands back and forth, massaging it. Until this time, the foreskin of Joy's penis was flexible. His red head was also big. Mala slid her fingers over it. She lay on the floor of the room and removed her lingerie. She was naked. She asked Joy to lie on top of her

Joy got on top of her. She asked him to place his penis between her breasts and move it back and forth. She squeezed her breasts and pressed Joy's penis with it. It was the ultimate for Joy. Her soft breasts touched his penis. It was a new experience for him. Mala was going to be his wife! This was an adventurous exchange, and she was nothing less than his past experiences. As she moved his penis on her breasts, she slowly moved her tongue out and licked the tip of his penis. It was already wet. For the first time, Joy had started to leak his white cum without fucking. This was from excitement. Mala realized it. She took his penis into her mouth. Joy ejaculated into her mouth and she took the entire thing inside. It was not the end. She knew there would be many instances and after marriage, still more.

Finally, Joy could make love with his girlfriend after many years. At least now, he was confident that he could lead a happy married sex life with Mala. But, this was just the beginning and the future was not visible at the moment. He was already in the grip of various sexual encounters. But Mala was love and sex.

Joy was still not able to figure out the difference. The climax of every situation and the intimacy in each was beyond his imagination. Every incident happened on the spur of the moment, it was a fatal attraction. However, Seema continued to remain in his mind. The scene he saw as a boy flashed again and again.

Was he leading a normal life? Was this a natural phenomenon or was it something specific only to Joy? A bright engineer by profession, he was technically very sound and was a System Engineer in a reputed organisation in New York. In the hustle and bustle of the city, Joy and Mala started to live together in the same apartment. It was a life that every New Yorker led. Yet to get married, both of them had their plans to be in India next year. Months passed by. Joy and Mala were in sync with each other. It was a relief to Joy that they were together and things were okay when it went back to sex. Unaware of what was coming next, Joy concentrated on his career and his career path was well defined. He was to be in a Management Course. Mala was happy with her job and was not very ambitious. Life was cool and a holiday was planned in the near future. It was winter and Christmas time. In New York, it was exciting, as Christmas Eve brought on festivity and lights. They had planned a holiday to the Niagara Falls and then a few more places. Both were excited to proceed with their holiday plans and spent Christmas in New York, the cold winter and snow. In the midst of all this, Joy was almost leading a normal life, when all of a sudden a call from India, flashed him back to the past. It was Seema, who had called from India. She was on the line with Joy's grandma. Joy was nostalgic and nervous. He had a strong inclination towards Seema and the relationship had no definition or place in society, it was all behind closed doors. "Hello!" as she spoke, her voice was low. She said, "How are you, Joy Baba?" Mala was also on the call, unaware of Joy's feelings. Seema was soft and emotional as she spoke. Joy realized that she was almost down with tears. It was difficult for Joy to work out this situation, it was just an infatuation and sex that Joy had with Seema, but he did have feelings for her. It was quite obvious as she had taken care of him as a boy and had given him all that he wanted. The conversation went on and Mala remained ignorant of the situation. Finally, the call was over and Seema was miles away from Joy. She remained in the same ancestral house where Joy grew up. It was Seema who had influenced Joy's life and he was living a life with experiences that were not common to every man. It was an urge that lead to ultimate satisfaction. Such traits are not found in every person. He was leading a life that was driven by sexual desires. It was a personality behind closed doors. Both Mala and Joy enjoyed their first Christmas in New York. It was filled with fun and frolic, wine and food.

They went for their holiday to the Niagara Falls. Everything went well and as Joy desired, leading a normal life with Mala. As the holidays got over, they were back in office and it was already mid-January.

The Trip

Joy was back to office. He was one of the most decent guys at work, and was adored by everyone. He was tall, fair and handsome, and in his mid- twenties. A career well balanced and a path defined, he was confident in every stride he took. As he advanced in his career, there was a change in the Management of his office. He was to report to Sharon, who had been transferred from their office in San Francisco. She was tall, almost 5'7" with a perfect figure and delicate moves. She had graduated from the University of Berkeley and was dynamic. Known for her managerial skills, she was the most wanted in the Management sector, with her professional qualifications and skills. She was also attractive and enticing, and in Joy's eyes, was even more so. He could not help it and it was his nature. His desires were drawing him towards her. One fine morning, Sharon came up to Joy and stood in front of him. As there was not much interaction between them, though Sharon was his Boss, he was confined to his desk. But, this time, the proposal was different. Joy had to travel to the client's site and now, it was Sharon who was to accompany him on the trip. She sat on the desk with a half skirt and a white top. Her dress was tight and stuck to her body. Her breasts were well-shaped, and there was a fine cut in the top in front, just in between her breasts, and her fine cleavage was visible. Her legs were white and her thighs had good amount of flesh on it. She wore high heels and her toes were well-shaped, nails well-manicured. As she sat on Joy's desk, her curves were prominently visible and her buttocks were on the desk. Amazed as he was, Joy was speechless. In a moment, she said hi, and laid the proposition for a business trip to the client's location. Excited as he was, Joy's eyes grew bright on hearing the proposition.

The arrangement and the presentations were made for the trip. For a week, they worked hard, staying late in the evenings. Sharon had developed a good professional relationship with Joy. The late evenings ended with coffee and dinner. Both had developed a chemistry that could present them well in front of the client. At home, Joy had maintained a normal relationship with Mala and life was okay. But his attraction towards Sharon was drawing him towards her. He had a different mindset, and it was playing on his mind every moment.

The flight and hotel arrangements were made and the destination was Miami. The meeting was fixed and the day had arrived to depart. The flight was in the evening, and Joy had taken a day off from office. Mala was back from her office to pack up for Joy. The trip was for a week. Mala did not suspect a thing about his fascination for Sharon. This was an art that Joy was good at. He was well in control of his feelings and not a clue could be drawn about his intentions. By now, Mala was almost living as Joy's wife. In the US, this was very common. She used to share all her experiences with Joy and expected the same. But, unaware that Joy was leading two lives, a life where he was known to be good gentleman with a strong character, and another life where he had sex with various women. It was time. Joy had to leave for his flight as Mala hugged and kissed him. Every moment she had with Joy was precious. She loved him and believed in him. There was very less time to reach the airport and Joy rushed to the cab. It was in the evening and the traffic was dense. However, Joy managed to reach the airport and Sharon was waiting for him. Dressed in a professional outfit and as a perfect corporate woman, she was particular about her presentation and timing. She was an experienced lady and had worked in the industry for quite some time. "You are late!" she said, as Joy rushed towards the ticket counter. Finally all formalities were done and both of them were at the departure gates. Sharon shared some of the highlights of the presentation with Joy and he listened to it with rapt attention. The gates opened and both of them walked into the aerobridge towards the aircraft, as they were greeted by the crew. Both of them sat beside each other. Sharon occupied the window seat and Joy was next to her. She looked smart and beautiful, and had blue eyes, rosy cheeks and pink lips. The aircraft was ready for take-off and within a few minutes, they were airborne. It was a three hours and ten minute long flight to Miami. They were served dinner, after which it was time for a nap. The lights went off, and the expected arrival time in Miami was around almost midnight. Within a few hours, the announcement for descent was made and the dazzling city of Miami was visible from above. The coastal belt was lit. It was the first ever trip to Miami for Joy, and with great excitement, he bent towards Sharon, who sat on the window seat to watch the city, which was one of the world's hottest destinations, famous for its beaches. The aircraft touched down and taxied to a halt. Both of them embarked on the aerobridge towards the conveyor belts to collect their luggage at the arrivals. A cab was already waiting for them from the hotel. As they drove from the airport to the hotel, Joy was thrilled to see the charismatic city.

In a few minutes, they arrived at the hotel. It was a beach resort. They had to spend a few days here for their presentation. It was already beyond midnight and they were escorted to their rooms. Sharon bid goodbye to Joy and retired to her room. As Joy entered his room, he found it to be spacious with a bed for two, a sofa and a study table with all kinds of amenities. Though it was time to get to bed, he was not getting sleep; he opened up his laptop to review the presentation. Restless as he was, his inner desires were tempting him for another act. Could he resist it? What was tempting him? Could he muster the courage to do it? It might cost his career. None but Sharon! He remembered his moments with her, and was craving to have her. He couldn't take it anymore and wanted some fresh air. The room had a sea-facing balcony and as he opened the glass doors, a gush of air blew into the room. It was a full moon night and the silver lining of the waves was amazing and beautiful. It was a refreshing moment. Joy took a deep breath.

Next to his balcony was Sharon's. He glanced at it and saw Sharon lying down on the chair with her eyes closed. She had changed into a sleeveless white silvery colour nightgown. Her long hair was flying in the air, sexy and beautiful as always. It was a scenic sight in the moonlit night. Joy was mesmerized by the two sights. For a few moments, he was lost. All of a sudden, he realized he was drawn away towards her. In the meantime, Sharon realized that she was being watched, and saw Joy gazing at her. She was shocked and got up from the chair. In the moonlight, Joy saw her in her night gown. It was transparent, so he could see the outlines of her curves. Sharon, though surprised, smiled at him. A matured woman, she realized that it was not the usual Joy standing in front of her on the balcony. There was no one on the beach and Joy pointed at the beach to Sharon. Sharon nodded and went back to her room. In a few minutes, both of them were on the beach and on the soft sand. They were speechless. Joy was spellbound. He dared to take a step that could cost him his job. He looked into Sharon's eyes. She was still. She touched Joy's hand and caught hold of it. She moved forwards and put his hand on her back. Her lips were wet and enticing. She kissed Joy's lips and held him tight and started kissing him. Her tongue was inside Joy's mouth. They were engrossed in each other. She had taken both his hands on her back and hugged him tight. It was a climax. Joy was at his peak. He held her tight and kissed her on her lips. Both of them were kissing each other and getting violent. In a minute, Sharon took off her night gown and stood naked. Her body was shining in the moonlit night. The sand beneath was glittering. As she stood naked, it seemed like the moonlit night had bestowed her with great beauty. A perfect woman that she was, she was well-shaped and her body was attractive as ever. As Joy kissed her, holding her tight to his body Sharon slowly moved her hands towards Joy's pants, to remove it. Both of them lost control. She stripped Joy naked. In a few minutes, she laid him on the moonlit beach. Joy's penis organ was erect and big. She slowly massaged it with her soft hands. She sat on Joy's legs. Her curvy and well-shaped buttocks were shining. She slowly slid Joy's dick into her mouth moved her hands all over his body and started playing with the hairs on his chest. Her saliva had made Joy's organ wet and as she removed it from her mouth, his organ shone, with the red head pointing at the sky. She kissed his balls, as she brought her hand down towards the lower parts of his body. She kissed his pubic hair, and sprinkled the soft sand on his body, and she spread it all over, and then gradually went down on Joy. She moved his dick onto her clean shaven pussy, brushed it over again and again, and then inserted it into her vagina. She moved up and down vertically. Her long hair slid on her back. It was the kind of orgasm that Joy had only dreamed of having, with Sharon. He was gasping and moaning as Sharon went wild on him. She took it in harder and deeper. Joy had also started to move in harder. "More! More!" she said and turned around. She went on digging harder. Joy's dick was wet by this time as she was wet inside. All over her body, sweat glistened. Her lips were watery and juicy. Joy moaned and all the blood rushed into his organ. He could not hold it in any longer. Sharon was wilder than any woman he had come across. She let it loose and the milky cum rushed out. She took it all over her face, on her breasts and everywhere else. It was rushing out. Joy wanted more. He did not want to stop, but it was over. She lay over Joy on her back. Joy slowly took his hands over her breasts and massaged her nipples. He pressed it hard and she felt pain. But not to end it, she inserted Joy's fingers into her hole and wanted more. It seemed that the moonlit beach was hot by this time. It finally ended and both of them lay down naked on the beach, until they realized it was nearing dawn. Back in Sharon's room, both of them took a hot shower. The night had passed and Joy's fantasy was fulfilled with Sharon. It was time for sunrise, and both of them were back in their respective rooms.

The alarm rang and it was 9:00 AM. Joy rushed for a shower and to get ready for breakfast and then the presentation. In a while, he met Sharon in the dining hall. She gave him a pleasant smile. "Are you ready?" she asked. Joy answered saying, "Of course! Yes." A new relationship developed between them. The presentation went very well. The chemistry was stronger. A professional and physical bonding between the two - but was it love? That was the question in Joy's mind. Was it about their emotions? The answer was no. It was sex. How long would it last? Would it last for moments like the others? The final day of the presentation had come to an end. Joy had another feather in his cap. Miami was another chapter to him. Was he getting into something we could define as an addiction? Or was this normal behaviour? Was he driven by basic instinct? Was it leading to a never ending story for him? There was no time to think. This was America and life was fast. It was a Saturday afternoon. Joy and Sharon were back in New York. Both of them went back to their normal lives.

Marriage

Two years had gone by. Joy and Mala had been living together. There was immense pressure from their family and friends, as they kept asking them to get married. Mala continued with the same job. Joy was in the same organisation and had gotten a few promotions. After all, the chemistry worked. Sharon now headed the entire division, having bagged the contract from Miami. Finally, Joy's and Mala's wedding was fixed, and was to take place in Mala's hometown, Delhi. The reception was to be at Joy's old zamindari house in Eastern India. Everyone was excited. Family and friends were invited. After two years, Joy and Mala were going to India to get married! They had taken leave for two weeks, to attend to the arrangements for the wedding. Most arrangements were made in advance by their families, only those for which their presence was required remained.

Their tickets were booked. As they packed their bags in their new apartment taken on a mortgage in Downtown, New York, Mala held Joy in her arms and said, "I love you!" It was a pleasant surprise for Joy. There was nothing new here. They had lived together for two years. Was Joy honest in their relationship? Did he have to tell Mala everything? Did she have to know about the other part of this life? Would Mala accept him, if she knew of Joy's experiences and his dark side? Could his sexual fantasies and experiences affect their life together? After all, they would be bound together in matrimony. Would he stop doing it? Was he a playboy? Was he a split personality? Was he leading a double life? Once they had packed, Joy and Mala finally boarded the plane to New Delhi. The plane taxied on the runaway, and was finally airborne. It was a long flight and it was wise to have a drink and nap. It was late at night in India as the aircraft landed in New Delhi. They completed all the immigration formalities and walked towards the arrivals after collecting their baggage. Despite being late at night, Mala's entire family was present to pick them up. Delighted to see them, Mala's father hugged Joy. "Welcome to India!" he said. Joy was thrilled with the welcome. They drove to Mala's house. The city seemed to have changed, with many flyovers having come up. It was hot in summer. It was the city where Mala had spent her childhood days. It was a nostalgic trip for her. The car entered the posh locality of Mala's residence. It was 3:00 AM by the time they reached. The jet lag had affected Mala and Joy. They needed sleep and were taken to separate rooms. This was India. Though they had lived together in the US for two years, it was not appropriate for them to share a room until after the wedding.

It was late in the morning when they got up. The house was bustling with noise as everyone was busy with decorations and music. It was a festive occasion and Joy was their hero. He was supposed to leave Mala's house officially and come from his home to get married to Mala as per custom. Joy's parents arrived late in the afternoon and there was lot of happiness in the air. Both families were together after a long time. Mala and Joy were the only children of their parents.

Joy's father had recently bought a posh bungalow in Delhi for the couple. In the evening, they drove to their posh bungalow, bidding goodbye to Mala and her family for the day. It took a while for them to reach the house. As Joy entered the house, Seema and his grandparents received him. His grandparents were old by this time. Seema was in her late mid-forties. She was like a family member to them. Joy bent down to touch his grandparents' feet. He had a soft corner for Seema. She hugged him. Her own son had grown up, and had also come down for the wedding. Seema's husband stood in a corner. "Joy Baba!" Seema said, and offered him a sweet. Tears trickled down her face as she greeted Joy and welcomed him back home. Joy was quiet. He felt her emotions. Seema was the beginning of everything! She wiped her tears and went to the kitchen. Joy's parents were equally emotional. He had grown up to become a successful man. Seema had contributed to all of it. Joy went upstairs towards his room. He turned around and saw Seema. She was the same woman who had shared everything and every moment with her. On entering his room, he found it was spick and span. Everything was well decorated. The bed was clean. Mats were placed on the floor. There were flowers all around. The room was full of fragrance. He realized that Seema had kept things neat. Joy's parents were both working, and did not have time to spare for Joy's needs.

The posh bungalow had an outhouse where Seema was to live with her husband. Her parents had permanently shifted to Delhi. Though the wedding reception was to take place in the old zamindari house in Eastern India, all arrangements were to be made from this very house in Delhi. Joy's room had a window that opened out onto the outhouse. Joy could see the lights on in the outhouse from his room.

It was time to take a bath. Joy refreshed himself and went to bed. It was early in the morning when Joy woke up to find that tea was placed on his bedside. Seema was standing right next to the bed. She was staring at Joy and watching his every move. He took the cup and began to sip the tea. "Joy Baba," she said, "You have changed a lot and become very handsome! How is life in the US? How are the people there? Do you miss India? Why do you not think of coming back to India?" There were many questions from her end. She put her hand on Joy's head and shook it, smiling. She played the role of a mother, partner and everything to Joy. She fulfilled every desire of Joy. She had made a sacrifice in her life, devoting herself to the family and Joy. Her son was now eleven years and was in Secondary school. Did Joy realize the love and Affection that Seema had for her? Or was it the sex appeal and the sex drive that dominated his personality? What was he today? Would it be acceptable to Indian society? Seema was not aware of Joy's other experiences. Was Joy's dark side visible to others? Many questions remained unanswered for Joy.

Meanwhile, the festive mood was on high in the house. The bungalow was decorated with flowers and lights.

The Great Indian Wedding, as it is called, unfolded with pomp and splendour. Friend and relatives started pouring into the Raichoudhury House. Joy's full name was Joy Raichoudhury. The sound of the shehnais, or the wedding trumpet music filled the air. Joy was the hero for the day. Friends and relatives poured in. Everyone was eager to see him. He had returned from the US and in India, it is taken as a matter of pride and adds to one's status. It was new and exciting for Joy. There were frequent calls from Mala on the developments at every stage. Mala was from Delhi and had more friends in Delhi than Joy did. They visited, too, and met Joy. Excited as he was, there was nothing stopping him from enjoying every moment. He was the Prince! The final moment had arrived. He got dressed as a groom. A professional makeup artiste and other assistants helped him get ready. But, Joy knew that whatever it was that he did, the final look could only be certified as appropriate by one person - Seema. He had to put on his Dhoti and Kurta. He asked the makeup artiste to excuse him, and called for Seema.

Seema entered his room on the second floor. Guests and relatives had gathered downstairs. No one was around in Joy's room. He wanted Seema's help. She put a gold chain around his neck and said, "For you!" Saving some money from her meagre earnings, she had bought the chain for Joy, intending that he put it on during the wedding. She adjusted the dhoti and tucked it in properly. She helped him put his kurta on. Finally, he was ready for the wedding. As Seema dressed Joy, she looked at him for a moment and burst into tears. She knelt down and took his hands and said, "I leave you from today!" She cried bitterly as she felt that Joy was being handed over to someone else.

There was no response from Joy as the poor lady sobbed in front of him. Did he have any feelings for her? Would he be able to narrate all that had happened to him? He realized that Seema was in love with him. It was a relationship that had no meaning in society. It could be termed illicit, even. He held Seema's hand and said, "You are my beginning!" Seema had dominated Joy's life. She had sparked off a side to his personality that no one knew about. She had sparked off the fantasies in which he lived, that drew him into relationships with many women. He held Seema for a moment and realized that he meant everything to Seema. Probably Mala would not be able to love him as much as Seema did. He would not be able to repay Seema by any means! It was selfless devotion by the lady. But would Joy change? Had he realized the essence of love? Could he develop that for Mala?

The answer was probably no. It was time for him to leave. He asked Seema to be by his side during the entire ceremony. Unaware of the relationship between the two, people had no question about Seema accompanying Joy in the car. Seema's parents were happy to see her going with Joy – to them; it was a bond that Seema and Joy had shared from Joy's childhood days. As the White Honda City pulled up outside Mala's house, Joy and his family were greeted with flowers and sweets. It was a festive welcome, typical to wedding ceremonies in India. Guests, relatives and friends were eager to see Joy. He looked handsome. There were smiles on the faces of young girls. The atmosphere was filled with happiness and joy.

Mala emerged from her room. She looked glamorous in her red saree as she approached the portico where the sacred mantras were to be read for the wedding, along with the "Hom," (a Holy Fire around which the bride and groom take seven rounds around, to solemnize the wedding). Friends and relatives sat around and people were taking photos and videos of the function. Joy and Mala took their place around the sacred fire, which in Bengali custom is the place where the sacred oath was to be taken to be honest to each other, to take care of each other and to be in the sacred bond of marriage forever. Mantras were read. Joy and Mala repeated them. Seema stood right behind Joy. Finally, the mantras were over. Joy's Dhoti was tied with a knot to Mala's for the "Saath Phere," (seven rounds taken around the Holy Fire). As they started to do the rounds, Seema moved away to a corner. She was holding back her emotions. From childhood to an adult, she had given Joy all that he wanted. Finally, there was nothing left to give. On the other side, Joy was smiling. He held Mala by the hand. They were celebrities for the moment at Mala's house. Photographs and videos and wishes were in the air. It was already late in the evening and time for dinner. Everyone went to eat, and with time, the crowd started thinning out. People left for home.

The evening had ended. On the first night Mala and Joy were to sleep in separate rooms, Joy was put up in a special room and Mala was in a separate one. Joy could not sleep. He was still excited. He sat by the window and noticed Seema in the courtyard. She was in her husband's arms, crying bitterly. Her husband held her close and was trying to console her. Feelings aside, it was difficult for Joy to understand what he was to Seema. In a few minutes, they left the courtyard and it was quite late at night.

Joy could not sleep. He remembered the past with Seema. The night passed and morning dawned. There were many rules that had to be obeyed as per customs. The day went on with more celebrations. That night, Mala and Joy were supposed to be together. It was not new for them. They had been living together for two years in the US. But now Mala was Joy's lawfully wedded wife. The door closed behind them, and outside, women were busy giggling. Mala went up to the bed. Surprisingly, Mala asked Joy, "Am I the only and the first woman in your life?" She should have asked him this before. But, there was a doubt in her mind at this point. What could have provoked her to ask this? Did she have a hint from Seema's behaviour? There was no chance of it at all! Joy was quiet for a while. He was afraid that he might upset and lose Mala if he told the truth. Instead, he asked, "What type of a question is this? You never asked me this when we were in the US!" It was impossible for Joy to tell the truth. There were many women in his life now. All his relationships were driven by passion and desire. He ignored her question and told her that they should sleep. He slept that night without touching Mala.

Next day, they had to leave for their old ancestral house in Burdhaman and they boarded the afternoon train. A few friends, relatives and Mala's parents accompanied them as they boarded the train. It took almost a day for them to reach town. As they reached town they were welcomed by the staff and gardener Kailash of the ancestral house.

Seema used to be careful while interacting with the gardener. Joy remembered the scene he saw long ago and realized that he had been affected that very day. He smiled at the gardener, and moved on. As they reached the palatial house, they found it was decorated in vibrant shades. It was late in the afternoon when they entered the palatial house.

Joy took Mala to his room, where he had spent his entire childhood. There were trees in the spacious garden. The house also had a courtyard. He took Mala with him and showed her around the place. She was thrilled by the place as she was from the city and had not experienced life in a town. The air was better and cleaner.

Soon, it was tea time and everyone was at the dining table for tea. "How do you like the place?" asked Joy's father, to Mala. "Oh! Fantastic!" They spent more time at the dining table. It was getting dark. The next day, there was a reception scheduled. Arrangements were made in the courtyard for food and drinks. There was ample space for a barbeque party. Joy's family was well-known in town. They were known for their celebration of festivals with pomp and splendour. The arrangements for the party were to be the best in the town. Joy's and Mala's parents left to visit the temple to offer rituals late in the evening with Mala. Joy was not interested in it, so he stayed back. He instead went to Seema's room to ask about the arrangements. It was a long time since he had been to her room. It was in the corner of the compound, and had a bathroom attached to it. The door was closed, but as Joy pushed it open, he noticed that there was no one around. On the bed, he saw Seema's saree and underwear.

He heard the sound of water from the bathroom. The bathroom door was latched from inside, but there was a slit from which one could look inside. Joy held Seema's saree and inhaled into it. He took her underclothing and inhaled the same fragrance that he had inhaled, years ago. Why was Joy so attracted to her?

Years had passed. He was more experienced and had been with many beautiful women. He went towards the bathroom and saw Seema naked. She was the same. He remembered every single incident and the precious moments that he spent with her. Nervous, he went towards the door and ensured that none was around. Seema's husband and son were in Delhi to take care of their house there. He took off his clothes and lay down on her bed, completely naked. The door opened and Seema was shocked to see Joy. She was naked and as attractive as before – just that she had put on some weight. She was a mature woman now. Joy had no time to lose. He got up and kissed Seema on her lips. She pushed Joy aside and said, it was not right for him to approach her for sex after getting married to Mala. Years had passed by and he was now in a different bond, and had to be mindful of Mala. Joy was defiant. He hugged Seema tight and started kissing her. Seema was almost in tears. She kept saying no again and again, but her weakness for Joy was immense. She was trying to keep away from his body. She urged him to let her go. Someone could come in! She said. But, Joy took her to bed and started sucking on her breasts. She could not control herself anymore. He took his hand and inserted it into her. She was seduced by Joy this time. In a moment, she opened herself and Joy took his organ and inserted it into her. She moaned as Joy pumped her. Joy pounded her harder and harder. He then took her from behind, her buttocks, now bigger and well-shaped. He started to lick and kiss her. Wild as he was, he was an animal by now. Seema had realized the change in him. It was not the same Joy. He was like a mad man. As moments passed by in the peak of the encounter, Joy could not hold on anymore. He ejaculated on her face even as she insisted that he not do so – to her, it was confirmed that it was not the same Joy Baba who had left town for his higher studies years ago. He was a totally different man. She held Joy close to her. In tears, she realized that something really was wrong with Joy. His body language had changed. She noticed that Joy was not in his senses and was driven by a strong animal instinct. After many years, Joy had hurt her with his pounding. She felt the pain in her lower abdomen. "Joy Baba," she said, "You are not okay!" Joy was back to his normal state and was unaware of what he had done to Seema.

It was time for Mala and his parents to be back. He hurriedly put on his clothes. Seema was nervous as she managed to get back into her saree.

By now, Joy should have realized that he was a different person, and that such sexual drives could lead to crime. Till now, he was lucky that he found women who liked him and gave in to his desires. Was Joy losing control? Was this leading to a personality disorder? A sex addiction? There were many unanswered questions in his mind. Would he have to go to a doctor? Seema had finished by then. She got dressed. She looked worried and stared at Joy. She knew he needed help. It was not the first time she had sex with him. As a matured woman, she could measure every pulse in the act and understood he had been involved with many other women. She was sad and blamed herself. All the effort in Joy's upbringing went in vain. It was dangerous. She could sense two personalities in him and the world outside was unaware of it. She still felt the pain in her lower abdomen. Joy left the room first and then she followed, putting things in the right places.

Who could she talk to about this change? If Joy's parents knew about it, they would blame Seema. She had to do something. It would affect Joy's married life if left unchecked! He was fond of women and more to them whom he fascinated. Mala arrived and Joy was a completely different man. He was jovial and enthusiastic. There was no sign of repentance in him. He was not nervous as he talked to Mala. She observed this from a distance. He had two different personalities trapped in one body.

Early next morning, Seema had placed tea near Joy's bed and stood by his side. She touched him to wake him up. He was almost awake and turned around. With a grin on his face, he took a sip from the cup. This time, Seema did not speak. She turned around to leave the room. As she was about to leave, she heard Joy say sorry. She turned and looked at him. The pain in her abdomen was still there. She was taking it in her stride. The reception was in the evening. There was a lot of work for her to do. In the meantime, Mala had arrived and stood at the door of Joy's room. Seema was cautious and pretended as though she was there just to serve Joy his tea. In the meantime, Mala sensed something fishy. She had known

Joy for a couple of years. His behaviour was different at times. There was no chance she could doubt Seema because of her age. This was to Joy's advantage. Seema was in her mid-40s and Joy in his mid- 20s. There was a huge age gap. She went up to Joy and asked why he did not go to the temple the previous evening. Joy shrugged and said he was not interested. Taking him by the hand, she pulled him towards her and asked if he was okay. She had a strong feeling that Joy was hiding something from her. What was it? She couldn't suspect Seema. Why did Joy seem strange to her, especially at this point when they were married and their reception was on the same day? Had Mala seen Joy making love to Seema? It would have been the end of everything! The stars were on Joy's side. He worked it out in a balanced way. For an hour or so, Mala was in his room and then left. Joy showed a sign of relief.

The Reception

All the preparations were made for the reception and the guests were invited. The entrance of the palatial house was decorated. A sign bore the words "Mala weds Joy." The house looked awesome, with the lights and flowers as decoration. A makeshift stage was prepared for the couple to sit on, and receive their guests. Everything was in place, but Seema was not to be seen anywhere. She was absconding from the scene as she had left the house, in the early hours of the evening and had not told anyone of her departure. Not even Joy's grandparents. Where could have she gone? Joy was already dressed in his suit and Mala was in her bridal saree. Both of them were on stage, as their friends and guests started pouring in.

It was a joyous moment and a matter of pride for the family to have both Joy and Mala well placed in their lives. It was a perfect match and the entire house was full with guests who had come to attend the ceremony. The courtyard was filled with guests who were praising the match. Joy's parents were proud. The same Joy, who had spent his childhood in town, was now an accomplished person in the US with a partner who was equally qualified and settled. Joy's grandparents relaxed on a cosy sofa that was placed right in the corner of the stage.

Joy was a bit uneasy. He could not see Seema. Throughout the ceremony, she was by Joy's side, taking care of him every moment. It was highly suspicious that she was suddenly nowhere to be seen. The thought that Seema might take some drastic steps haunted Joy. The day before, he had forced Seema into the act. She was not willing to partake in it. Her facial expressions in the morning showed that she was not happy. She was no longer just the maid; she had now become a family member. Eventually, intimacy had developed between the family and Seema. Joy's father called for Seema. When it came to their notice that she was missing, the rest of the family wondered where she had gone. Mala was surprised to see Joy's family asking about Seema and sending the rest of the staff to search for her. The house was empty. So was Seema's place. Joy left the stage and moved to Seema's room, where he had forced her to have sex with him last. As he entered the room, he found a note. Seema had written that she was leaving them and going back to Delhi from where she would take her family and leave. Shocking as it was, Joy began to act on it. He headed for the railway station right away. In the meantime, Mala saw Joy moving out of Seema's room. She followed him without telling anyone. Her heart was thumping fast. She had guessed something that she did not want to be true. Was it Seema that was responsible for the change in Joy's behaviour? She had noticed it for the first time during the ceremonies. Would she confront him to find out the truth? Mala followed Joy, unnoticed.

By this time, Joy had reached the railway station and was asking around about the next train to Delhi. Fortunately, there was none in the next four or five hours.

Impatient and nervous, he headed towards the platform. To his relief, he saw Seema sitting on a bench. Without a word, he stood in front of her. She was unmoved and was a statue. Joy held her hand, and it was cold. "What is wrong with you?" asked Joy. She was not willing to speak. Mala had arrived at the station by this time and was watching the entire scene from a corner. Joy had never seen Seema in this state. He had seen her being the kind of person to respond to everything that confronted her. Within minutes, Seema was in tears. She said, "I am worried about you, Joy Baba. Had I stopped you the first time, you would not have become an animal today." She was hurt and she knew that Joy had had a couple of experiences with other women. "Tell me everything," she said. It was already late at night. For a town like Joy's in Eastern India, there was very less thoroughfare on the platform and it was almost empty. There were a few lights with which Seema's face was visible.

Mala was nervous. She was watching Joy and Seema together. What could the relationship between the two be? From a distance, she could not hear much, but she saw both of them approaching the exit. She hid herself and followed them as they moved out of the station. Joy was intelligent. He maintained a distance with Seema in public. He was well-known in town. He belonged to an elite family. He walked with Seema on the road until he reached a deserted park. Both of them stepped inside the park. There was a bench to sit on. Joy sat beside Seema on the bench, unaware that Mala was right behind them. By this Mala had understood that Joy had a very sensitive relationship with Seema. What was it? She wanted to hear everything from both of them that very night.

The Confession

Joy held Seema by his arms as they sat beside each other and started narrating his experiences. As he spoke, all of it struck Mala like a thunderbolt. She could hear everything crystal clear. Never had she been suspicious about anything with Joy, but here she was, shocked out of her wits with the truth on the day of her reception. He started with his experience when he was eight, which he had once mentioned to Seema. But he had not told her all of it. He remembered every act till date. Seema was shocked to find out that Joy had seen all of it, and she was helpless. Joy convinced her that it was not her fault. He hugged her to console her and kissed her. Mala was out of her mind hearing and seeing all of this.

Joy then described how he was driven towards Seema after the day she had sex with the gardener. He had gone to school with all the excitement and desire. With such repeated encounters for years, Seema had made him a man at a very young age. He mentioned that he was fascinated by every aspect of Seema and how her body was precious to him. He mentioned the encounters. He told her about how he sucked her bottom and hairy pussy, went on top of her to bite her nipples and played with her body. Seema was speechless and found Joy in a different state as he narrated every single experience with her.

By this time, Mala was in tears, she broke down. Never had she thought about the other side of Joy's personality! But, she was deeply in love with Joy and was now bonded with him by matrimonial ties. Revealing Joy's relationship with Seema degraded her. Joy had not stopped and continued to speak and then went on to narrate his experiences in the train with his teacher, and how he had spent his time in the bathroom of a moving train. He ended the narration with his encounters with Sharon. He did not mention Mala. All of this was unbearable to Mala and she ran away from the place towards Joy's house, bursting into tears as she ran on the road. Her world had gone upside down and there was nothing left for her to live for. She was just about to begin her married life and had to hear all this from Joy's mouth!

Mala rushed to her bedroom from the backyard of the palatial house, unnoticed by anyone. She locked the room and sat quietly on the bed. But she did not lose hope and was sure that Joy was addicted to sex and he needed treatment. She was a woman of substance and was educated. Defeat was not acceptable to her. She decided to be the Seema for Joy and that very night they would be spending the night in the same room. Less than an hour later, she heard someone knocking on the door and was sure that it was Joy. As she opened the door, to her surprise she found Seema with him. Joy seemed vexed and tired. He wanted to speak up as Seema took Mala's hand and placed it on Joy's. She told Mala to take care of him. Seema had decided to leave the family and Joy did not stop her.

It was late at night, but Joy had no intention of going to bed. He was restless and lay down on the bed. Mala had changed into her night-dress and looked at Joy bravely. He was totally unaware that he had totally exposed himself and that Mala had found out about his dark side. She sat down behind him and asked how the day was. There was no answer from Joy. He was quiet. In a moment, he caught hold of Mala's hand and said, "Help me!" Mala pretended to know nothing and waited for him to speak up. Joy broke down and started with all that he had told Seema. Mala burst into tears. She could not control herself and revealed that she had heard everything. Joy promised that he would put an end to everything, and that it was Mala who was in his life now. It wasn't easy to digest everything, and Mala suggested that Joy visit a doctor, take some expert advice and mend things.

Joy was not okay with her suggestion and insisted that she believe in him and take an acid test. Both of them were emotional. Mala realized that the only way to have Joy was to give him the sexual pleasure that he desired. She had to be the best mate for Joy, and not let him think about others. She was a woman. What Joy was seeking in other women could be found in her alone. She was open to any kind of sex that he desired. She closed the doors of the room and removed her night-dress. She stood naked in front of Joy and kissed him. Joy was not ready for her. But Mala knew that she had to be the ultimate seductress to him. She kissed him all over his body and began to seduce him. Joy was hesitant to do anything about it. Mala had made up her mind. She had to get Joy involved. She took off his shirt. She kissed his hairy chest and touched him with her hands. She moved onto him and took his hand, to put it over her breasts. "Please," she said, "play with them!" Joy could not resist any longer. He went wild and pressed her breasts. He sucked them hard. Mala was at the peak. Her naked body sprung into action. She moved her bottom on Joy's penis and began to rub it hard. She took off all of Joy's clothes, by now, he was naked. His penis was erect. It was the same story. He brought Mala closer to his mouth. Mala sat with her pussy on Joy's mouth. He started licking it. It was wet. She moaned as he bit her gently. He caught hold of her buttocks and started licking her anus. He was wild and did exactly what Mala desired. She took Joy's finger into her mouth and sucking it. With her other hand, she held his dick and massaged it. They were deeply engrossed in the act. Mala turned around and started to give him a blow job, while Joy was licking and sucking her pussy. She moved her body and inserted his penis into her vagina. She was doing exactly what Joy had been describing to Seema. These were his experiences with other women. Mala wanted Joy's lust to get out of his system. She believed that giving Joy an active sex life and doing it exactly as Joy wanted would stop him from going to other women. Not only that, she was also thinking of taking the help of a counsellor for Joy. By this time, Joy was pounding Mala hard. She bore the pain. He hurt her, wild as he was. Her muscles were strained and she took all the pain silently. "Give me more!" said Mala. Finally, Joy ejaculated into her vagina. She sighed in relief and kissed Joy on his lips. Both of them were tired and drifted off to sleep.

THE DEBATE

It was late in the morning when Joy and Mala woke. When she got up, she kissed Joy and went to refresh herself. She had taken a lot more than usual last night, and her muscles were in pain. She could feel it as she walked towards the bathroom. She opened the shower and took a hot water bath. She had many things to do and Joy was her priority. Relatives and friends were leaving after the reception and Mala wanted to discuss everything with Joy's mother. These things were better handled by women than by men. She wanted to see how she could place the issue, and how such matters were to be kept between the husband and wife, and had to be sorted out carefully.

First, Joy's parents would not believe this, and their relations could be strained. Joy's parents would never believe it because he was a totally different person to the outer world. No one would believe that Joy was addicted to sex. It could lead him to seek paid sex and illicit relationships with other women. She had to move fast and was thinking about how to go about it all. He had to be taken to be a doctor. Should she wait for some time and then take a step? She finally realized that she had a friend in the New Delhi who could help her.

Was it a disease? Surely, this could only be determined by someone who had experience in the field. Was it common to other men? Of course, all men do not have so many relationships. She felt that all this had happened because of what Joy saw at the age of eight. There needed to be a change. How to do it was the question. Mala called her friend in New Delhi. She was a doctor and Mala consulted her, intending to narrate Joy's experiences right from his childhood days. She wanted to discuss every incident and his relationship with Seema, knowing that such relationships in the future would affect their married life. Mala called up the number from the landline of the palatial house. The voice on the other side was gentle and soft. "Hi!" Mala recognised her friend's voice and responded immediately. Both of them were thrilled to talk to each other after years. Mala's friend was an established practitioner in New Delhi for quite some time. She had a good circle of doctors who could help. Mala described the situation to her friend and sought her advice. She wanted to know whether they had to go to a doctor at all, or whether this could be rectified without intervention. She described Joy's childhood and other incidents. Was it normal? Or did these events actually have a tremendous impact on his personality? Mala told her friend that he was a normal man and that he was very different to the outside world. Could this spoil his reputation? It was a matter of his life and career!

Her friend understood the situation well. She responded saying, it could be seeing things that should not be seen at a young age had affected Joy's character and personality. For this reason, he was driven by a desire for sex. She also mentioned that having wild sex did not mean that a man had personality or disorder or that he needs counselling. He had sex with women at their will, and they had sex with Joy because they liked it themselves. It could be considered as natural, that they had shared. Joy had not committed a crime like raping a woman or forcing them to have sex.

According to the Priya, there were many agencies in Delhi who offered paid sex and that it was a thriving business in the city, with high profile girls and women being involved. Customers were well placed businessmen and high ranking officials. Mala was not convinced by this. But, she was not only talking to a doctor but a friend who was putting across the practicality of the situation. Mala's friend asked her whether she liked Joy in bed while having sex. Mala had no answer. Joy was the perfect man. He was used to playing with her body and giving her the ultimate satisfaction. Mala had been with Joy for years and she also realized that Joy had never forced Mala to have sex. He could have done it with Seema who was always in his fantasies. Women enjoy sex more because of better orgasms. She was defiant while speaking to her friend and was not able to understand what she was trying to point towards Mala. She was afraid of losing Joy. He had not committed a crime but had been in relationships with many women. It could be because of his personality. But, could this be accepted by any married woman, knowing that her husband was prone to having sex with multiple women? Was this adultery? She had many questions. She could not express it to her friend on the phone.

On the other end, her friend was offering her an insight into very practical situations. Her friend wanted to meet Joy. She also mentioned that many men had casual sex and after that, they forgot who it was they had sex with. They went about, leading their normal lives. Society had accepted it and everything was hidden. There were no proper rules. Most Metros today thrived with social and adult clubs where men and women had casual sex. But, would Joy be one amongst these men? Was it such a common phenomenon that it led to the creation of spaces where women went onto taking up high profile prostitution?

So far as Mala knew, Joy was never into all this. He had just acted based on his imagination and fantasies. Being a doctor, her friend clarified that it was Seema in Joy's mind always. The child brain is always receptive and absorbs very fast. What Joy saw at the age of eight was by accident. It was unfortunate that he had seen such a scene. Seeing the naked body itself tends to arouse a feeling and an attraction, which is common both for men and women. It was a long conversation and there was no end it. Priya was also married to a well-known doctor in Delhi. She said that medication could change Joy completely, it would totally submerge the sexual urge but had side effects, and he could be a totally different man and could be dull by nature. It could affect his thinking and his intellect could be destroyed, therefore before taking a decision to put a person under psychiatric treatment the pros and cons should be seen. It was not easy. What was being discussed had the criticality in terms of putting a bright and successful man under treatment.

Was this desirable? As she put down the receiver, Mala understood that it was a difficult task to solve the puzzle and she had to wait for more time to have Joy under treatment. Engrossed in her thoughts, she sat in a corner in the courtyard. Stakes were high and Joy's life could change in total, if given the medication it could affect his personality. She was totally confused. If he was referred to a doctor in India, then in the US, it would be difficult to continue the treatment.

It was only Mala who could change Joy. The counselling and the mentoring had to be done by her. It was afternoon. She was lost in thought as Joy came round. He sat beside her and said it was time for them to be back in the routine life in the US. She nodded as she got up to go for lunch, without uttering a word. She was tired and could not take all of it. It was just the beginning of their married life. The situation was different from what it was a day ago, unaware of all that had happened in Joy's past. She decided to meet her friend before leaving for the US. It would be better if she could have Joy join her, so she planned a get-together with her friend's family.

Soon, Mala called Priya, and Priya understood that Mala was impatient about the entire situation. Mala wanted to introduce Joy to Priya. She needed some feedback from her. As a doctor, Priya could judge Joy's character. But, Joy had maintained all his incidents as a secret and had only told Seema about them, that too, after many years. He made sure to balance both sides of himself. The day passed by for Mala as she was lost in thought. It was time for them to leave. They had a break in Delhi and then had to take a long flight to the US. All of them had to leave together, even Seema. She bid farewell to the old house for the last time, knowing that she would never come back. So much had happened in the last two days that had changed Seema's and Mala's lives. It had turned Mala's life upside down. All of them were normal in front of Joy's and Mala's parents. Joy's grandparents stayed back in the house as the others left to the railway station.

The Get-Together

After a day, the family reached Delhi. Seema had expressed her intention to leave the family to Joy's parents while travelling on the train. They did not agree, as she was the one who had taken care of the lavish bungalow in Delhi. Joy was quiet through it all. Once in Delhi, all of them sat in the spacious drawing room of the house in the evening. Joy's father approached Seema's husband and asked him to stay back, unaware of the weird reasons that made Seema so determined to leave. Even Mala's mother held Seema's hand and requested her to stay back. She said that there would be no one to look after Joy's parents.

Seema also owed a lot to the house and the family. They had provided her with all that she wanted from the day she began working in the house in her early twenties. Finally, she agreed to stay back, knowing that Joy was leaving for the US in just three days' time. Mala was not happy about this, but understood the fact that Joy would be living with her in the US. It was time for dinner. As usual, Seema got busy with all the preparations. Mala's parents gifted told Seema that they would help her son and her if she needed any financial help. Seema did not need it. She was well paid by Joy's family and had all the freedom, as though she were a family member herself. Dinner was served. All of them sat at the dining table. Mala revealed her plans for a get-together at her friend's place the very next day. They decided to make it an overnight sleepover. Priya had invited Mala to stay back after dinner. It was late at night when dinner ended and everyone went to bed. Back in Joy's and Mala's room, both of them were casually talking to each other. The lights went off and both of them went to sleep.

Both of them got up early in the morning and had to finish their pending work in India before leaving. They had a couple of official appointments in India. After spending the whole day with government officials for different formalities, they were back home in the evening. Mala had packed some gifts for Priya and kept some nightwear aside for herself, to spend the night. Both Joy and Mala drove to Priya's posh apartment. They were given a warm welcome. Priya was happy to see Joy with Mala. She was impressed by the first look at Joy. He was tall, fair and handsome. He was attractive and charming. She found him to be jovial and enthusiastic.

Mala made it a point to observe Joy and Priya keenly. She had actually brought Joy along so that Priya could assess him and give her honest feedback. She served both of them some whisky and the four of them began discussing various topics. Joy was a good orator and though quiet in nature, he had the ability to pull the crowd towards him. Priya's husband was a doctor. He shared various experiences from his life. Joy shared some of his own experiences and talked about life in the US, their trips to the Niagara Falls and other places in the vicinity. He managed to charm Priya and her husband and drew their attention. When they started drinking, it was already late in the night and Priya's husband had gone over his limit. He decided to call the get-together off for the night, and went to sleep. Mala was tired after a long day. She ate a bit and went to sleep.

Priya and Joy stayed awake. They were talking right into the early hours in the morning. By now, Priya wanted to go to bed. Joy was also about to leave when Priya caught hold of Joy's hand. Joy was nervous and he knew that this would be another experience for him. He hesitated a bit, but Priya wanted it that day. She pulled Joy's hand and put it into her panties. Joy felt her hairs. He massaged her, and pushed deeper. He inserted his fingers into her vagina. Meanwhile, she began massaging Joy's dick over his pants. She stood up and ensured that the doors of both bedrooms were locked. She removed the laces of her red night gown. Priya had heard about Joy's wildness from Mala. She stood naked in front of him.

Joy removed his clothes and stood up to hold her. He held her bottom and pressed it hard and put his mouth on her nipples. She was excited. Joy began sucking and biting her breasts. He took one leg of hers and put it over his and pressed her against the wall for support. He inserted his penis into her vagina and started fucking her hard. He pounded on Priya and she enjoyed every moment of it. She turned around and asked Joy to fuck her from behind in the doggy style. He moved back and forth, and thrust into Priya's wet pussy. She enjoyed every moment and then kissed him on his lips. Finally, she took Joy's cum into her mouth. It seemed that she wanted Joy to unleash his sexual desire, forgetting that he was her friend's husband.

It was already the early hours of the morning and they were both refreshed and tired. They both looked into their bedrooms to find that Mala and Priya's husband were asleep. A hot early morning shower would be a catalyst to a good sleep. Both of them got together for a shower in the bathroom and enjoyed the bath. They hugged each other, naked, in the bath, and kissed. In a few moments, they joined their respective partners and went off to sleep.

COUNSELLING

It was late in the morning the next day as everyone got up from bed. Everything seemed to be normal as before, Mala and Priya's husband unaware about the incidents that happened between Joy and Priya. It was time for Mala and Joy to take leave and Mala was eager to take some suggestions from Priya and her feedback about Joy. She went to up to Priya when she was alone in her room. Upon entering the room Mala cautiously asked Priya how she felt about Joy with the entire activity last night. She was interested to know if she could proceed with some kind of counselling initially and if required to go with medication which was preferred to be the last option.

Priya was quiet for a moment and then responded. She said that Joy was normal and his sexual drive was a different aspect which could exist in any individual. She also said that it was not predictable how Joy would react if taken for a treatment. On the contrary he should be ready to accept that there was some problem in him and that had to be rectified. All the sexual encounters had taken place with the acceptance from the women that Joy had sex, there was no forced sex, Priya as a woman was satisfied with the entire experience with Joy the night before. She had taken the advantage to satisfy her sexual needs with approaching Joy for sex. Mala realized there was not much to be gained in the conversation with Priya about Joy getting medical attention and left the room. In the meantime Joy was having a good time with Priya's husband and they were engrossed in a discussion. She interrupted them and insisted Joy that it was time for them leave.

By afternoon, Mala and Joy left Priya's house and reached home. Preparations were on the way for them to leave for the US and Mala had to act immediately. The only way out was to counsel Joy herself and then go to a doctor. She felt that no doctor would play an active role until and unless Joy himself admitted that there was a problem in him and that his sexual drive could have a negative effect on him. But, how to put it to Joy, this was not an easy task and had to talk upfront with him. Joy was busy with the packing as Mala approached him and requested him to spare sometime alone with her. She stressed that they had an important discussion. She then asked Joy how was the experience in Priya's place and how did he spend time in their house. Joy answered back saying that everything was fine there and he had a wonderful time with Priya's husband and Priya. Mala was unaware of the entire incident that took place in Priya's house and acknowledged Joy's reply. But, she wanted to start the discussion with Joy on the past sexual encounters and if he would try to rectify himself. She started the discussion from his experiences with Seema and said that she wanted to understand how he got so much inclined towards Seema after seeing her in an act when he was in the tender age of eight, it was an age where children would not be able to understand such incidents. Joy was a bit surprised that Mala had started with a topic in the midst of the preparations for them to return to the US. He was very cool and answered back saying that it was like a real life movie to him, though he was eight he was attracted by the entire scene, it was a feeling that could not be explained. She indicated to Joy, it was high time Joy realized that things were not normal with him and there needed a correction with some counselling that would help him to rectify himself.

Intense sexual contact with various women could also cause diseases and it was not a healthy practice to get involved with so many women and having sex with them. She gave all the options to Joy whether he needed a doctor's attention or she could help him with various counselling sessions avoiding any medication. The motive was to control Joy's intense sexual desires and with various women.

Joy agreed to get counselled by Mala and have daily discussions with an additional initiative to get into meditation and give some time to spirituality out of his busy schedule. He was suggested by Mala to draw his attention towards documentaries and books that could clear his vision and his thoughts about women, so that he could control his sexual drive, though Mala knew that she would also need Joy as a partner where love and sex would have a primary role for a happy married life.

Preparations for leaving to the US were over and finally the day had arrived for them to fly back to the US. As they left their posh bungalow in Delhi, Mala prayed to

God that the next time she came back to India, she would bring back a different Joy, a completely different man and his attractions towards Seema would have diminished, Joy would only be hers'.

They reached the airport and after clearing all the formalities they were ready to board the aircraft. Mala was a different woman now and she had promised to herself that she would change Joy. In a few moments that gates opened and they boarded the plane. The plane was ready for take-off and after a few minutes they were airborne.

After a long flight they landed in the US and took a cab to their apartment. It was a Sunday and they got back to their apartment to unpack and settle things. Mala made it a point that she would have two sessions with Joy every day, in the early morning and before going to bed in the night. After the day's work though tired she called Joy and requested him to have a session with her. She wanted to know how he felt the entire day and his thoughts, Joy was normal and answered that he was OK. She then concentrated to have him meditate and concentrate with eyes closed for some minutes. Joy did as Mala said and started the practice of meditation.

Months passed by and Mala changed Joy's habits gradually, early in the morning he was habituated to meditate and before going to bed. He had started reading spiritual books and gradually he felt that his vision was clear. He was not fascinating women the way he did before and his perception had changed. He felt he was a changed man and Mala had brought the entire change in him. He was now dedicated to his work in the workplace and back home gave his quality time to Mala.

After a year, there was good news and Mala was pregnant, Joy was going to be a father and he knew that by this time he had turned to a perfect family man. After a few months the new member in the family arrived and they were filled with joy. There was happiness in the family and Joy lead a normal life with wife and kids. In a few years the couple was a part of the elite society in the US and Joy was now a matured man, not driven by fantasies. He was thankful to Mala for everything.

Mala was convinced that Joy had changed and kept her promise that her next trip to India would have a completely different man in Joy.